Freddie the dragon was a creature of old,
A creature whose tale has never been told.

He lived in a land so far, far away,
Seeking adventures day after day.

Dragons, you know, from their mouths they breathe fire,
But Freddie was different with a problem so dire.

He was different you see and it made him quite glum,
'cause poor Freddie's fire came out of his.... bum!!

FREDDIE FIRE BUM

Written by
KEVIN BELL

Illustrated by
SARAH-LEiGH WiLLS

From all other dragons Freddie wanted to hide,
For being different like this, he just couldn't abide.

They called him bad names which made him feel numb,
They laughed, shouted and sneered - "It's Freddie Fire Bum!"

He asked to be normal and cried to his dad,
He asked why he had such a problem so bad.

His mum and dad told him that it mattered not,
That flames hot and scary fired out of his bot.

They loved him regardless, they loved him so dear,
They said to ignore all those dragons who sneer.

But to Freddie those comments, just weren't right,
When all that he wanted was to be a brave knight.

He wanted to be a dragon knight like his dad,
And protect his village from those who were bad.

But the dragons who laughed said it wasn't for him,
Which made Freddie feel worse and totally grim.

He wanted to shout that life just wasn't fair,
But just then he noticed a dark cloud in the air.

That dark cloud drew closer and soon Freddie could see,
Dragons so scary, he wanted to flee.

The dragon knights of the village, did try to fight,
But against these new dragons, they just had to take flight.

They flew to escape the fierce dragons' sharp jaws,
But against these new creatures they stood no chance because...

When they did try to flee, the fierce dragons thought yum,
The fierce dragons flew up and bit hard on their bums!

The village knights couldn't fly and turn to breathe fire,
So it was Freddie they called for and did really require.

Freddie swooped down and the fierce dragons gave chase,
To eat little Freddie it was almost a race.

But against *his* fiery bum they just couldn't get near,
As Freddie pumped fire, crowds started to cheer.

The fierce dragons gave up and decided to leave,
As a win against Freddie, they just couldn't achieve.

Now our Freddie's a hero and his parents are proud,
"It's great to be different!" were the shouts from the crowd.

To the village, our Freddie, he did so inspire,
And now all of the village wants a bum that shoots fire!

So you see if you're different, please don't be glum,
As our hero was different - our little Freddie Fire Bum.

FOR HOLLY, EMILY, JESSICA AND AVA

FREDDIE FIRE BUM

ISBN: 978-1-9995856-0-0
Published by Gilded Unicorn publishers.

Illustration and design by Sarah-Leigh Wills.
www.happydesigner.co.uk

Printed in Great Britain
by Amazon

51026037R00017